Conversation Starters

Smriti Malhotra

Ukiyoto Publishing

All global publishing rights are held by

Ukiyoto Publishing

Published in 2023

Content Copyright © Smriti Malhotra

ISBN 9789360164614

All rights reserved.
No part of this publication may be reproduced, transmitted, or stored in a retrieval system, in any form by any means, electronic, mechanical, photocopying, recording or otherwise, without the prior permission of the publisher.

The moral rights of the author have been asserted.

This book is sold subject to the condition that it shall not by way of trade or otherwise, be lent, resold, hired out or otherwise circulated, without the publisher's prior consent, in any form of binding or cover other than that in which it is published.

www.ukiyoto.com

Acknowledgments

At the outset, I would like to express my immense gratitude to God who has made me capable of writing my thoughts so beautifully.

Individually, I want to thank for the support and inspiration to; my parents, Vinod and Veena Malhotra, my brother Chirag Malhotra and my husband Arun Vohra. They are the pillars of my life and today I am standing strong because of them. They have always supported me in achieving my dreams and motivated me to move an extra mile.

Romila Chitturi, my mentor, editor and proofreader, to whom I am truly indebted. She understood everything I was trying to accomplish from the first day the idea of writing this book came to my mind. From ideas to introductions, conceptualization to creativity, engaging to editing, she was there for me 24X7. Her contribution to the book is truly incredible and valuable. I might have written the content but it was her idea to create this insightful book out of it.

It took an immense amount of work to bring out this book and it would not exist without the invaluable contributions and assistance of a few relatives and friends. I can't mention everyone but yes would like to name some for sure: My Nanka (mother's side), My Dadka (father's side), My In-Laws (husband's side), Unicorn Team, Shavy Verma, Edouliu Riamei, Geetika K. Bakshi, Nehal Lala, Divya Singh, Nancy Chaudhary, Monika Ahuja Malik, Ruchi Kalia, Pallavi Sinha, Sandeep

Das, Saurabh Saluja, Priya Saluja, Ankit Chaturvedi, Arpita Dhawan Chaturvedi, Shubham Chaturvedi, Manasi Bhatnagar, Kapil Choudhary and all the people who have been always there with me in all my ups and downs.

Forewords

It is my pleasure to introduce you to this captivating, insightful and thought-provoking non-fiction book titled "Conversation Starters" penned by Smriti Malhotra over a span of a few months. Smriti has meticulously researched and compiled information that is both informative and thought-provoking, providing insights and new understandings. Her new book has presented a comprehensive and well-rounded perspective on women, mindset of today's generation and much more. Her work is definitely going to challenge your assumptions and broaden your horizons. With its engaging writing style and attention to detail, it promises to be a page-turner that will leave you enlightened. Through the use of real-life examples and personal opinions, Smriti has created compelling and accessible narratives that will engage and inform readers of all backgrounds on some of the burning and current topics. Be prepared to have your preconceived notions challenged and your understanding of life, relationships and some harsh realities will surely get expanded.

- Romila Chitturi, Entrepreneur, Hyderabad

Since the time I have been reading Smriti's writings, I have only seen her grow exponentially as a writer. From writing poems with a romantic undertone to fabricating brief pieces around social issues, especially those that concern women, I have been a witness to how she has fully tapped into her talent. This book by Smriti is just another excellent example of her knack for writing, and I'm sure that every reader will gain something valuable from their reading of this book. I wish Smriti all the best for every future endeavor.

- Nehal Lala, Editor & Content Writer, Delhi

It's been more than 6 years since I met Ms. Smriti Malhotra, with captivating dreams of becoming a successful writer. She is living her dream and bringing up the vital problems of the society related to different aspects of life, especially women. This is her first non-fiction work and I love this to every extent. These writings will provoke you to ponder a bit more about the general issues around you and definitely take some necessary actions towards them.

- Geetika K. Bakshi, Author, Blogger & Language Interpreter, Delhi

Smriti, as her name refers, is unforgettable because of her unique personality. I have never met her in person, but through her virtual avatar, she personifies a kind human being. And that's exactly wrapped up in her writings. She is a go-to person for adventurous experiences and social involvement with elegant proficiency. I can certainly vouch for her awesome work in anything, whether it be a blog, a poem, an article or even a book. What I like the most about her, is her way of

learning for the best rendition, which literally reflects in her work. So, if she is going to write another book, that too on personal experience, trust me, it will be a blast for the audience. All the very best my dear friend for enriching the readers' stuff with your classic sauté in your upcoming book.
- Preity Rashmi, Software Engineer, Pune

I came across Smriti Ma'am in 2022 through Unicorn Magazine. Her designing as well as writing skills are always fantastic. I often read her blog posts and poetries which she posts on her social media handles. Her writing style is unique. She is an inspiration for all the young writers like me. There's a lot to learn from her. I am sure she will definitely amaze everyone with her new book. I really hope her words will continue to encourage people.
- Rishu Sharma, Writer & Psychologist, Ranchi

Smriti is a dreamer. I still remember my first meeting with her around 5 years back where she said my dream is to become a writer and I could see that shine in her eyes while sharing her dream and today when I read and see her achievements. It just brings so much joy and pride in our eyes as a friend. I am sure this is just the beginning.
- Saurabh Saluja, Entrepreneur, Delhi

Just wanted to share a bit about how you have progressed in your thoughts and your dreams . I almost check all your poems, writings and articles and it does speak your mind and heart. Perfect

combination of the mind meeting the heart. What I like is, you're honest and straightforward in expressing your thoughts. Wish to see more of you through your writings.
- Arpita Dhawan, Entrepreneur, Delhi

About the Book

I am very sensitive about women and social issues, and one day I decided to pen all my feelings. In the book, you will find various issues that are impacting society as a whole. Every chapter flashes a different perspective and will surely make you fall into the thinking zone. This book is very special to me as it's my first book in the non-fiction genre. While compiling this book, I have been on a roller coaster of sentiments.

Readers, are you ready to be touched by the real experiences? I am sure after reading this book you will be in search of answers to a lot of questions.

Happy reading!!
Smriti

Contents

Chapter 1	1
Chapter 2	3
Chapter 3	5
Chapter 4	8
Chapter 5	11
Chapter 6	14
Chapter 7	17
Chapter 8	19
Chapter 9	22
Chapter 10	24
Chapter 11	26
Chapter 12	28
Chapter 13	30
Chapter 14	33
Chapter 15	35
Chapter 16	38
Chapter 17	40
Chapter 18	42
Chapter 19	44
Chapter 20	46
About the Author	*48*

Chapter 1

Has Anyone Decided The Retirement Age For A Housewife?

"A woman also gets tired, she also feels hot in summers and cold in winters. She also gets old and a helping hand from her family (especially men) is required!"

25,35,45,55,65,75 and if alive till 85 a housewife works, works and works. We have a retirement age decided for everyone but did someone ever think of a retirement age for a housewife??

I wonder where they get the power to do the entire household chores single handed. I have witnessed houses where the men of the family don't even bother to take a glass from the kitchen and expect the women to do everything even when she is not well.

The Indian culture of women doing all household work needs amendment!

India is famous for its cultures and traditions but there are some traditions which need amendment now. We have been taught in schools that both men and women are equal, then why there is a difference when it comes to household chores. I don't expect the men to do everything but a little help is not much to ask for. If the men can't help, at least they should not increase the burden on the women.

People should understand that a woman is not a wonder woman but a normal human being. If a man gets tired after working the whole day, a woman feels the same too.

My friends have sacrificed their passions as they are responsible for all the household chores

I am not forcing my opinion on anyone but I am sure there are a lot of women out there who can relate to this. I have seen my friends who have sacrificed their passions and dreams just because the family told being a woman they are responsible to do all the household chores single-handedly.

I believe not everyone's the same, there are families who support too but there are some who don't pity the woman ever during her menstruation. While she is bleeding and bearing so much pain already, she is expected to do everything as usual.

Just for once, imagine the same thing happening to a man and I bet he will not be able to even stand on his feet. India is westernizing everything, so why is a man cooking and helping his mother, sister and wife considered abnormal?

I really want everyone to understand that a woman also gets tired, she also feels hot in summers and cold in winters. She also gets old and a helping hand from her family members (especially the men) is required!!

Chapter 2

A Flight That Made Me Realize The Significance Of Food!

"Seeing food being wasted on flights aches my heart, there are still so many people in our country who cannot afford a meal a day!"
I visited Bangalore through Air India and during this journey, something caught my attention and I thought to write about it.

Food is one of the most important things in our life. It is basically the thing we work for. Keeping aside all the wants and luxuries in life, food is perhaps the most important as it is required for our survival. During my two way trip, I saw my co-passengers wasting food. I am sure we all are aware of how difficult it is to have food onboard. There is so much hard work behind it from cooking to packaging to bringing it to flight finally to the passengers.

I don't know what people expect to be served on a flight

While traveling to Bangalore from Delhi, there was a young couple sitting adjacent to me. Since it was a morning flight, breakfast was served to us. It was a pretty decent meal – a coleslaw sandwich, a vada accompanied by vegetable curry, a corn patty and a piece of chocolate brownie. Honestly, I had the meal and the taste was reasonable but the couple beside me took one spoon of each and then left saying salt is less, there is no taste, it's cold and many other things too.

I mean – you can say NO directly before taking the meal, at least someone else can have it. I don't know what people expect to be served on a flight; Butter Chicken, Paneer, Dal Makhani and Naan. Seriously, it really annoyed me. I am not judging anyone here but I guess we all should understand how lucky we are to have food, a couple of times a day.

I have realized that wasting even a small grain of food is a sin

A similar thing happened to me while I was going back to Delhi. A woman and her daughter were sitting beside me. Lunch was served to us as it was an afternoon flight. What the woman did was really appreciable. She only took 2 things that she could eat and said no to the rest of the dishes on the plate. On the contrary, the daughter took the whole meal and did not eat it. I guess the mother can understand the importance of food and she showed it too.

I have witnessed such incidents earlier too but why I felt like sharing it now is because I have realized that wasting a small grain of food is a sin. I saw a post on social media where a father and his 3 years old daughter were doing a roadshow. They were performing a balancing act. He was holding a long stick and his daughter was on the top. The only difference between the father and daughter was hunger. Be grateful for the food you are getting and try not to waste any of it!!

Chapter 3

The Moment I Realized His Fear Was So Much More Than Mine

"We often tend to confuse fear of marriage as nervousness but a guy I met helped me understand the reality." I had been seeing guys for marriage for a long time and somewhere deep inside, I always had a fear; a fear of commitment, a fear of responsibility, a fear of losing my freedom and what not. I thought my fear had reached its maximum limit until I met this one person who changed my perception.

I met this guy almost six months back through a matrimonial group and we spoke for less than twenty minutes in our first meeting, as it was with parents and I'm sure you all know how matrimonial meetings can be! Later, when we met alone for a second time, he shared with me his fears of marriage for the first time. I thought it was cool and even though I was scared, I still had the courage to make this decision. I thought he'll be fine once he gets comfortable. But to my surprise, we met almost 5 times and nothing changed.

It wasn't that he didn't like me. He spoke to me properly and he did confess that this was the first time he had met someone for 5 times but he was still unable to make up his mind. Even though our meeting was arranged by parents, there was some connection that built up over time during these meetings.

When he finally said no during our last meeting, I started seeing other guys again. But after two months, he texted me all of a sudden and asked me to meet him. I met him because I never forgot about him. We met again, had our favorite coffee, went for a drive and he seemed a bit more positive. Due to his fear, he asked me for 2 more days and I thought it would be a yes for sure since he himself showed up this time.

Shockingly, he still told me that he is confused and doesn't know what to say. I was so mad that I asked him directly about what it is that makes him so scared. I told him that I understand marriage is a huge decision, but even though I am scared, I'm still ready to do it.

I was very anxious and since he was unexpressive, it took me a lot of time to make him comfortable so that he could share his thoughts. Finally, he told me that he is scared of responsibilities and commitments. He shared that today, he is free to make any decisions without thinking twice as it's only him, but after marriage or kids, he needs to think twice before making any decisions. I realized this fear is deeply ingrained in him that even love, friendship or comfort cannot take it out.

I share this incident because we often hear that he or she is scared of marriage and we take it very lightly. But I think that a lot of the time, we tend to confuse that fear with nervousness. I can say that I actually met

someone who is so scared to get married that I realized that I was only nervous and not scared.
The biggest takeaway from our last marriage was that I realized his fear was and will always remain more than my fear.

Chapter 4

My Parents Asked Me to Remain Quiet, No Matter What Happens!

"My father always taught me, be it a love marriage or arrange marriage, the first three years are a locking period. Every girl has to do a lot of adjustments!"

It's been three months since I got married, and many might think that it's too early to write on this topic. Therefore, I am not writing about my marriage experience, but something which I was taught before my marriage to have a successful life ahead.

India is considered to be one of the fastest economies in the world, but still has a stereotype society that stinks. A society that will make you realize and remind every day that you are a girl, and you should learn to live that way only.

Being born in a liberal home didn't help

Thankfully I was born and brought up in a family where equal liberty was given to me and my brother, but when I was about to get married everything changed overnight.

Whenever I sat down with my parents, they began to teach and tell me things which were unacceptable.

My father always taught me, that be it a love marriage or arrange marriage, the first three years are a locking period. Every girl has to do a lot of adjustments, and it will be nothing new for you!

Patience is an enforced virtue

Be patient no matter what happens, you don't have to argue or answer back. Eventually, with time, everything will fall in place.

My mother didn't give me any different advice. Whenever I shared my fears with her, she told me that silence is the best solution to all my future problems.

She shared her journey with me and how being quiet helped her to complete thirty-three years of marriage. To my surprise, when I shared my thoughts with other close members of the family, everywhere I got the same reply.

But till this date I didn't understand why I was asked to remain quiet?

It's the girl who has to undergo the biggest change after marriage, it's a 180 degree shift for her and still people expect her to remain silent. I don't want to hurt someone's feelings, but this is the wrong advice parents have been giving to their daughters before getting married.

I don't say they should encourage her to misbehave or fight without a cause, but they should encourage her to at least put her point. They should teach her to raise her voice against injustice, to never allow anyone to hurt her integrity.

Parents need to do better!

Parents should teach their daughter to answer back when someone speaks roughly and is rude when it's not her fault, for that reason it may be anyone.

In India, the biggest fear for parents is their children getting separated or divorced, and this fear is instilled deeply in them that at times they give wrong advice that not only makes their daughters silent for a while but sometimes for forever.

Chapter 5

Kerala HC Contradicts Itself In 2 Verdicts On 2 Consecutive Days: So Is It FOR Women's Rights Or ANTI Women?

"I mean seriously, how can you blame a girl's dress for someone's unwanted gaze and comments? As much as I was amazed with the first one, I am more ashamed reading the second one."

I recently read two decisions made by the Kerala High Court. Honestly till yesterday, I was really appreciating the respected court for the first decision but when I read the second one today, I was really disappointed and heartbroken.

Verdict 1: 'Husband's Repeated Taunts, Comparisons with Other Women Qualify as Mental Cruelty'

At the outset, let me share my opinion on the first one which was, "Husband's Repeated Taunts, Comparisons with Other Women Qualify as Mental Cruelty".

I mean just read the verdict again – I was really so happy about it that I wanted to write about it and share it with the whole world.

You might have heard or read, "dusro ki biwi zyada acchi lagti hai', (wives of others are better)! This is usually said in a fun way, but some men take it literally.

It doesn't matter how beautiful your wife is, how qualified she is and how impressive she is, some men are never satisfied. I really don't have to go far to experience that, I have witnessed this at my own home. "Kuch seekho usse" (Learn from her!) is the basic dialogue of such men! It's a big torture is to listen such taunts on a daily basis.

In the movie Taare Zameen Par, Aamir Khan tells a story about a tree in a village. The villagers wanted to get rid of the tree but they couldn't, so every day they would come to the tree and abuse it immensely, and one day the tree would die. This story states that the words are often enough to kill someone, and taunts are big torture for anyone. The word mental cruelty is apt for such taunts and the comparisons made.

Once again, I really appreciate the court's decision.

Verdict 2: 'Sexual Harassment Complaint is Invalid if the Woman was Wearing a Provocative Dress'

Coming to the second decision which I read today, which just blew my mind. It said, "Sexual Harassment complaint is invalid if woman was wearing a provocative dress".

I mean seriously, how can you blame a girl's dress for someone's unwanted gaze and comments? As much as I was amazed with the first one, I am more ashamed reading the second one.

I am sure this would have shook the girls of Kerala and other states too. I wrote a blog that now it's time for India's people to upgrade their mindset; I think they are just busy upgrading their phone's software.

I even hate to think that just because I am wearing a midi skirt or midi dress, boys have the right to say anything to me. India might be a free country but the women of India are still chained. As though India's people were not enough to make women feel insulted, now a respected court is doing the same too?! Why should I think 100 times about what I should wear?!

The right to freedom gives citizens basic freedoms with respect to speech and expression, to form associations, freedom of personal liberty, freedom to live a life of dignity, etc but where is our personal liberty from among these? In fact such decisions give liberty to the wrong people to do whatever they want.

I think every decision has an enormous impact on society. Where one decision gave utmost respect to women, the second one took it back.

Chapter 6

To What Extent Would You Go To Fulfill Your Desires Or Dreams?

"People can lose all reasonable thinking and their present life too, for a few moments of gratification. No dream is so big that it can cost the life of a person."

I watched Delhi Crime (Season 2) and to be honest there were a lot of things that hit me. Like the shortfall of police force, denotified tribes being targeted, working women being accused of not balancing their family.

But the biggest one was to what extent people can go to fulfill their desires or dreams.

It's a show, but has a kernel of reality

Although all of them are serious issues for society, every issue needs to be taken care of at different levels. I know it is just a web series made for entertainment sake in which some hypothetical things are also shown, but ask yourself aren't these incidents a harsh reality?

Everyone wants a luxurious and better lifestyle; the desire to achieve this is sometimes so much that the way to achieve it doesn't matter anymore, as if people are possessed by it. Someone said rightly, "everything has its pros and cons" — where the improved lifestyle has brought a transformation; there it has also increased crime in the country.

*Spoiler Alert

Shortcut to becoming rich?

Season 2 is about a girl who works in a beauty parlour. During visits to her rich clients houses she gets a burning desire to open her own parlour. The lifestyle of her clients fascinates and she begins to lust after a similar lifestyle. And to make this happen, she chooses to walk on the path of crime, as a shortcut to become rich.

Unfortunately I have experienced this in my family too. I met my cousin (maternal uncle's son) recently, and he told me that his friends have iphones and ipads but my uncle doesn't buy him anything. So he stole money from my uncle's wallet. That's his first step towards crime.

There is so much comparison amongst children that unintentionally they get attracted to the wrong ways to fulfill their desires. It's not necessary that a crime needs to be big, even a small stealing from parents wallets and purses can lead to bigger crimes in future.

Film and TV actor from the US Lana Parrilla says, "There's always going to be someone who is prettier than you, better than you in some way, but everyone has something that makes them different." Another statement I came across was, "Comparison is the thief of Joy," often credited to Theodore Roosevelt. I feel both the statements are self-explanatory; just to have a few moments of luxury, people lose their present life also. I am sure no dream is so big that it can cost the life of a person.

Chapter 7

Loving Adults — Love Is More Dangerous Than Its Reputation

"The Danish web series Loving Adults, on Netflix, starts with a powerful fact—Almost all murders have something to do with love. Almost!"

I am really impressed by the themes depicted in the web series nowadays. Most of the shows created are very relatable. The era we live in is complicated and confusing, and these series help us explore the grim part of human relationships.

Our minds think beyond imagination, our actions are unpredictable, and we are ambiguous.

My article is inspired by the web series I saw recently, Loving Adults. The series opens with a disclaimer that reads in the start, "all the characters and events depicted are fictitious. Any resemblance to a person living or dead is purely coincidental".

People don't want to love, people want to control

The Danish web series on Netflix, starts with a powerful fact, "Almost all murders have something to do with love. And it's almost always about jealousy and passion." Emphasis being on almost, and love.

Love has become more than a feeling, it has converted into craziness, stubbornness and obsession. And fictional depictions on different media mediums, lived stories and news around us have turned love into craziness. People don't want to feel love, instead they want to control love.

The web series talks about a married couple with a 20-year-old son suffering from life-threatening illness, and the husband has an extra marital affair.

Murder is a grave crime

The story revolves around the same, and at the end it leads to a series of serious crimes. I understand that cheating is awful, but killing someone is a bigger crime. Murder is a grave crime, far more serious in degree than cheating on a life partner.

People can't accept rejection or losing to someone. Every day we witness certain bulletins with respect to this topic and sometimes the reasons are not justified.

Reading such topics is disturbing, but unfortunately this is the reality of life. As I mentioned earlier, our generation is really incomprehensible, and you can't foresee what's going on in one's mind.

Jealousy is a double-edged knife

Jealousy has become very common. It is destroying lives daily. The web series were entertaining in the past, but today they have turned factual.

I really appreciate the mind of creators that through these web series they are helping us to become aware about the serious criminal and social issues of the society, as it says "prevention is better than cure".

Chapter 8

Insults And Regular Taunts Can't Drive Person To Suicide: Really, Mumbai Court?!

Honestly such verdicts leave me speechless!
Before I begin to mention the whole case in details, I want to mention the definition of the words "insult" and "taunt" to bring to the notice that sometimes they can be mental torture.

Taunt – a remark made in order to anger, wound, or provoke someone.

Insult – speak to or treat with disrespect or scornful abuse.

I will be quoting the exact news for reference.

Taunts and regular insults mere "daily wear and tear of family affairs"?!

The court made the above said observation while acquitting 30-year-old Prashant Shelar and his 52-year-old mother Vanita Shelar of the charge of abatement to the suicide of Prashant's wife Priyanka. "The daily wear and tear of the family affairs wherein mother-in-law sometimes complains that her daughter-in-law does not work properly," additional session judge NP Mehta said.

According to the Hindustan Times report, Priyanka died of suicide on January 16, 2015, within a month of her marriage with her boyfriend Prashant.

"The said factual circumstance cannot be termed as causing mental cruelty because it is a natural phenomenon and the same could be seen generally in this stature of the family to which both parties belonged," the judge added. Further, the news says that Priyanka was not allowed by Prashant to talk with others on phone; it "cannot be a circumstance to infer that she was being harassed mentally," the court noted. Really? #Facepalm

So my first question here is, did anyone witness what kind of taunts were delivered to the deceased??

I would like to add from my personal experience that people take these daily taunts as a very 'normal', regular affair. Tells you how deeply these abusive behaviour patterns are ingrained in us. But how anguishing these are, only the person tolerating them can understand.

I don't know how the law works here and what the punishment could be, but giving such a verdict in the words it was framed, encourages taunting.

Every newly married woman needs a time of adjustment

As mentioned in the news, it was only one month of marriage, the first month the woman tries to adjust in the new house, with the new people, new environment and new ways of working. If she keeps receiving taunts and insults, can you imagine how she would feel?

I am sorry to say this but a man can never understand this thing because nothing changes for a man, he still lives with his parents, follows the same routine, but for a woman everything changes.

In India, women have been fighting for their rights since ages but now giving an observation that the regular taunts and insults are normal; I don't know what message the esteemed court is conveying to the society. For me, it's another step towards creating a destructive society.

Chapter 9

Didi, My Generation Wants Sex But They Don't Really Understand Intimacy!

I have seen a lot of people feel uncomfortable sharing their age, but I have no such hesitations. I am 32 years old and my younger cousins tell me that I belong to the 'old generation'. If you are born in the year 1990, you are still considered among them, but if a year less – 1989, you are from the old school.

Being an elder sister, my cousins come to me seeking advice about studies, career and relationships, but when I try to help in the way I understand, the only reply I get is, "Didi, leave it, you'll not understand it. Aapki generation aur hamari generation mein bahut fark hai. (There's a lot of difference between your and my generation)."

Is it really such a wide gap of thought?

In the last few days I was having a conversation with my younger sister about relationships, and she said something which hit me hard. Though she is from the new generation and I am from the so-called old generation, we share a lot of mutual thoughts and interests. We spoke about love, how the generation born after the year 2000 perceives love.

Her friend broke up recently and she shared the incident with me.

But first, let me say this – my words or I don't intend to hurt anyone or offend, it is purely an expression of my own thoughts.

Love in the past equated with loyalty, but nowadays love is often synonymous with lust, and maybe just sex. She shared the story of her friend whose boyfriend cheated on her while being in a committed relationship with her.

My sister shared her fear of loving someone or getting into a relationship. My generation had this problem but I guess the proportion of people was less. She asked, "Didi, what if the same thing happens to me?"

When you feel like an older soul between your peers

To be honest, I had no answer and I was completely quiet. After a pause, my sister said, "Didi, I feel I have a generation gap with my own generation."

I asked her, "Why do you say that?"

She replied, "My generation wants sex, but they don't know the real meaning of intimacy." It was really deep what she said, and I understood her point straightaway. I remember a thought I scribbled in my diary which read, "Everyday relationships die, because they are merely a lie." I felt the same a few years ago, when I was looking for love which I never got.

I asked myself many times where the problem is… After many years, my little sister gave me the answer. I had it too – this generation gap within my own generation!

Chapter 10

Celebrate The Baby Steps That Made The Person Who You Are Today!

I am mentioning my age again, and I am not at all ashamed of writing my age publicly. I am 32 years old, and would say being a part of this generation all these years were not at all easy.

Parents' pressure of securing good marks in school, getting admission in a good college, attaining a good job, relationships, heartbreaks, profits, losses, marriage; I think I have seen a lot and sometimes even more in all these years.

Looking back, I realized I did achieve a lot!

Today when I look back I realize I have achieved a lot, I have brought a lot of change in myself in terms of physique, confidence or professional learnings. Still, sometimes I get the feeling I have done nothing.

As I shared in my earlier blog, I have been getting a lot of inspiration from the themes depicted in OTT platforms, hence here comes another one.

I think you will agree to the fact that we all keep running behind big successes and ignore the little achievements we attain in day to day life.

A small step at a time takes us to our goals

Yes, I am talking about the baby steps that we take on a daily basis to reach our destination. I mean, waking up early in the morning is itself something to celebrate daily.

I remember an instance; while I was at school I struggled to pass in Math subject in my 9th grade, and somehow when I was promoted to 10th grade, I was afraid, as a student has to secure above 80% in Maths if he/she wants to opt for Commerce with Maths in 11th grade.

This is one incident I always remember because someone changed my life back then.

I got enrolled for a Maths tuition and my sir encouraged me to solve only 2 questions per day. Not only that, he used to give me chocolate for solving the questions. I shared with him my fear, he said be happy that you at least solved 2 questions and let's celebrate this first.

We should not forget the baby steps!

As I moved on in my life, I forgot to celebrate the baby steps I took later. When a child is born, parents celebrate the baby's first step, and I feel it is equally important for us to celebrate the baby steps/little efforts we make to convert our dreams to reality.

For each individual baby step can be different, but the most important question is are you celebrating that baby step you took may be after facing immense fears.

I guess every day will be a celebration if we start acknowledging the baby steps.

Chapter 11

Last Week I Booked An Uber Auto And I Was Surprised By What Happened...

Last week I booked an Uber auto from my office to the Central Secretariat (CS) metro station, and during my journey a pop up came on my phone that really surprised me.

Before narrating the whole incident, I would like to state that there have been a lot of harassment cases reported against Uber/ Ola drivers, and women's safety is a major issue.

I had an unpleasant experience with Ola a few months back

I booked a cab from Taj Palace to my residence in North Delhi. I got into the cab at 10pm and the driver dropped me at home at 11:45 pm.

Firstly the driver was drunk. Secondly he took a longer route and then he started racing with other cars. Then he intentionally stopped at a CNG pump at 11:15 pm, owing to which I had to get down at an isolated place, that too when I was in a short dress.

Anxious during the whole journey, I was on call with my brother and kept reporting to him about my whereabouts.

After that incident, I stopped using Ola and have been using Uber since then. I will not blame the company on the basis of the behaviour of a single driver, but yes the fear that instilled in me is still fresh.

Compare that with what happened when I booked an Uber

Now let me share what happened on 16th September 2022.

It has been raining in Delhi continuously for 2 days and we all know what happens to the traffic then. It comes to a standstill.

I had booked an Uber auto to Central Secretariat metro station. As we crossed Shantipath (famous as the Embassy Area) we got stuck in traffic.

The auto didn't move for almost 20 minutes and immediately a pop up came from Uber. It stated, "Need help? Your vehicle has been stationary for a while. Please let us know if everything is OK". The message was followed by many options.

I was really impressed by this new update by Uber. It is a major step taken towards the safety of women.

There was a headline lately that said "Delhi is not unsafe for women!" Such measures will reassure women that they are safe while traveling in cabs.

Chapter 12

Somewhere We All Are Scared!

The inspiration behind my blogs and poems are my personal experiences which I come across everyday. I feel if you have been through something, or felt it to your soul, you can pen it better as it comes directly from the heart.

Recently, I watched the series "Wedding Season" on Netflix which is about arranged marriages and the fake profiles parents make on matrimonial sites for a suitable match and what happens when the truth comes out. Though I will not be writing on this, while I was watching the series, I heard a dialogue to which I relate closely and what this blog is about. "We all are scared".

I mentioned about the generation gap within our generation in my last blog, I would continue this to it. Our life is not only complicated but full of fears and the worst part is that the fear starts from our childhood. In the past people were not very modern but they were carefree. I remember my father used to say, "Beta acche se padhai karo fir party karna, then acche college mein admission lo tabhi acchi job milegi, acchi job loge tabhi accha life partner milega" and this cycle never ended.

What fears do we face everyday? Fear of not getting good marks, fear of not getting admission in a reputed college, fear of getting ditched, fear of marriage, fear of rejection, fear of commitment, fear of failure and so on. I will go back to the series where the girl expressed, "I am scared of this marriage" to which her sister replied "We all are scared" as she got a promotion and had to shift to London for her new role. Our fears might be different but the feeling is the same.

I don't know whether I am right or not, but these fears have possessed us to such an extent that they are taking over the lives of people. People are committing suicide because of fear. I have seen a lot of people asking questions to God like why only me, what did I do wrong but trust me majority of the population wakes up with different fears every morning. Some are scared of their job, their bosses, family members and partners. Most people think web series are a waste of time and are just for entertainment purposes, but I have learnt a lot of lessons from them. And my lesson from the wedding season was that we all are scared deep down but we need to be strong and keep moving. Don't let your fear overcome your life.

Chapter 13

Why Should My Opinions As A Writer Be Dictated By My Marital Status?

Being a writer is not easy, and I realized this long ago, but today I can feel it every day. Whenever a thought pops up in my mind, it's difficult to control myself from not writing it down.

I am sure all the writers reading this can understand my point, I seriously feel so restless until I puke everything on the paper that's going on inside my mind.

I began writing almost two decades ago and since then there has been no stopping. Likewise, I have been writing poems expressing my happiness, sadness, anger, love, hatred, anxiety, frustration and much more.

In the past, nobody questioned me about my writing, but today it is completely different because I am married.

I understand that life changes after marriage and we women experience different emotions every day, but everything I write is not based on those emotions.

A conversation I didn't want to participate in

An incident happened to me within just one month of marriage. I wrote a short poem about my mother and the day I published it I got a call from one of my father's colleagues.

This is exactly her words to me, "Beta dekh bura mat maniyo but ab teri shaadi ho gayi hain and aise posts acche nahi lagte. Log pta nahi kya sochenge. Main tereko likhne se nahi rok rahi, par zara soch kar post kiya kar".

Which thus translates as, "My dear, don't mind my words, but now you are a married woman. Writing such posts doesn't reflect well, people might judge you. I am not stopping you from writing, but please think before posting your write ups."

This is just a small part of the conversation that I mentioned here, though she explained it to me for a really long time over the call.

Why are my writings being questioned just because I am married?

I am not blaming her here, but I want to express how people's thinking changes after marriage. I have my own life, too, apart from being a wife and daughter-in-law.

Yes, out of 100, 95% things might be related to marriage and the rest of the 5% is my own. Not just me, but one of my writer friends experienced the same situation after her marriage.

A writer has the full right to pen down whatever she feels.

Honestly, if you are not a writer, you can't understand the anxiety bumbling inside when the thoughts remain unwritten. It is very important, especially in my case, to write as I attain mind and soul peace through writing. I feel a sense of stability after putting all my thoughts on paper.

Dear society, especially the ignorant aunties and educated uncles, please understand not everything is personal, sometimes it is just a normal happening around us.

Chapter 14

Didi, I Don't Have Expectations, I Have Requirements!

I met my cousin lately and yet again she said something which was really thought-provoking.

A lot of you related to the blog, Didi, My Generation Wants Sex But They Don't Really Understand Intimacy!, and the inspiration behind this blog was my cousin. In the last blog, I wrote that our generations don't have that much gap, but now I think we do.

Since I got married this year, and we were having some conversation regarding my expectations, she said, "Didi I don't have expectations, I have requirements". I didn't relate to it at first, but when she explained it to me, I was blown away with her words.

"An expectation is something hoped for, whereas a requirement is something that is demanded, something that is necessary."

Please read the above quoted sentence twice.

None asked me about my requirements

I remember when I was meeting men (the matches) for marriage, everyone asked me what are your expectations, but nobody asked me my requirements.

When expectations are being conveyed, you are indirectly making the other person the decision maker.

I mean, it's okay if he/she fulfills your expectations or not, irrespective of how important they are to you.

My cousin told me the time has come where girls don't have expectations, but requirements.

Today's girls know their value and won't settle for compromise

She, herself, told me, "I am very clear what I require from my partner and the same will be conveyed to him. I don't want him to take me for granted."

I mean, think to yourself, whenever we say I expect you to take me out, we aren't giving him the option?

Whenever I have a dialogue with my cousin, I feel elated to acknowledge the thinking process of girls today. They know their value, and they are not ready to compromise by degrading it.

Once again I would request to read the difference between expectations and requirements, and judge yourself is it necessary to convey your requirements or not?

Chapter 15

A Man's Infertility Is Kept Hidden Whereas A Woman's Is Announced Publicly, Shaming Her

I'm writing this inspired by one of the webseries I am watching currently. I will reveal its name in my next piece – for the moment, let it be a mystery.
My father taught me that education plays a very important role in the life of an individual; it crafts your thoughts, endows insights about a subject and creates awareness. Today, I could relate to every word he taught me.
Women blamed for not having a child even if the husband is infertile
People (here I am not only referring to the middle or lower class but also the higher class) are so insensitive that if a woman is not able to conceive they will always blame the woman and not the man.
Sometimes parents are even aware about it but they refuse to accept and continue blaming the woman. To add to the problem, if she conceives and gives birth to a daughter, the blame is again dumped on her head, despite the well known scientific fact that the gender of a baby depends on the man's chromosome – X or Y – that the fertilising sperm carries!
I would like to ask, why a son's infertility is hidden by parents, whereas a daughter in law's infertility or

incapability is announced publicly? I am sure a lot of you have heard this word "baanjh" which a childless woman is usually referred to.

When most families only want an heir from a daughter in law…

Becoming a mother is a dream of most women I guess, experiencing the beautiful journey of nurturing a life within you, and if a woman is unable to do so, it is already an excruciating agony for her and the society add's to it by their taunts and harassment.

I am sure you all have witnessed such incidents wherein a woman was blamed and the man was not even asked for a medical test. A dialogue from the web series actually pushed me to write on this subject. It said, "Am I valued only if I have a child?" Seriously, I have experienced that in some families the only thing they want from a daughter in law is a male heir and they go to any extent to get it.

Couples forced to have kids by family before they even bond

I have also heard somewhere "pehle pati patni to ban jaaye fir maa baap banenge" (can they truly become husband and wife before they become parents?") and it's so true. It's very important for a couple to first live the relationship of a husband-wife and sometimes in this spree of having grandchildren; the relationship of husband-wife is ruined.

I work with a diplomatic mission and I was told by one of the diplomats (an official representing a country abroad) that India is gaining power in all aspects but needs to pay attention to aspects like religion, caste discrimination, and gender equality – to name a few. I would once again like to reiterate that my intention is not to hurt anyone's feelings or offend them, it's just that when I come across such topics I feel it's better to bring them out as it might bring a transformation someday.

Chapter 16

Hush Hush: Is A Warning To Women Daring To Challenge Powerful Men

In my last blog about infertility, I didn't reveal the name of the series from which I got the inspiration to write, as I didn't complete watching it while I wrote that piece. My blog is influenced by the end of the same series.

I was watching "Hush Hush" on Amazon Prime, and I must say it's a pretty interesting one.

Just to give a gist, the series is about four best friends and one of them is murdered because she decides to expose some of the influential people who were involved in trafficking of girls, and she was also being convicted for the heinous crime. The rest 3 friends interrogate and dig in, bearing an endeavour to prove her innocence and not letting her sacrifice go to waste. It is still believed that women are built to stay dependent on men.

Though I don't want to break the suspense but still I would like to mention, the culprit turns out to be an influential man, and he says,

"The evolved, self-actualized women will never accept that they are physically, mentally and emotionally weak; they don't stand a chance against men. They always need the support of their husband, son, father or brothers. Their strength isn't their own, it is borrowed from us."

Honestly, a lot of you might feel this is not relevant here, but for me, it is.

Is the result of crossing the limit really an end?

I know it's just another series, but the message it conveyed at the end is that if a woman tries to go against men, the result can be really worse. In the series, Ishi (the character's name) tried to expose the so-called powerful men, and her life was ended.

Today also, if a woman tries to speak up, especially when she is expected to remain quiet, she is considered to be rude or insane. A woman is expected to follow the same paths created for her since ages, and if she decides to take a diversion, everyone makes a dead end for her.

Season 2 is awaited.

Chapter 17

Can The 'Reset & Recharge Break' Meesho Gave Last Month Be Replicated By Other Employers?

By God's grace, I have never faced the haunting 'corporate pressure'. I worked in a corporate company for a limited time and since then I have been working with a Diplomatic Mission, commonly known as Embassies/High Commissions. There have been times when I was overloaded with work, but there was never work pressure on me.

I have friends working in the corporate sector and I have been listening to their work pressure stories/incidents.

Last month, I was traveling to Faridabad to celebrate Rakshabandhan and owing to the festival, the metro was packed heavily and I couldn't move a step. With me, a young girl boarded the metro from the same station. She started cursing her company and 2 more girls joined her at the next station who I heard were abusing their seniors.

The whole journey I could only listen to "koi nahi samajhta, chutti ke naam par maa mar jaati hai, salary to badhani nahi hai, jitna karlo inke liye kam hai". (They don't understand; we have to create lies like "my mom passed away" to get our rightful leaves! They just make us slog, and don't ever think of increasing our salary!)

I am not blaming them but I know there is a lot of pressure on the employees and a lot of times their families have to bear their frustration and anger.

In September, Meesho, an Indian e-commerce company had announced an 11-day companywide break for all its employees giving priority to mental health in times when mental health has become a major concern across all age groups. This initiative is named "Reset and Recharge Break" allows employees to completely unplug from work and prioritize their mental well-being.

In an earlier blog, I had mentioned that Uber brought a new feature for the safety of women and now this initiative by Meesho. I am glad to witness the policies made by companies for the good of the people and not only products. It is an imperative step towards the society and I am sure a lot of companies will have such breaks for their employees in times to come.

Chapter 18

S3 Of Four More Shots Please! Leaves You With A Confusing Aftertaste

The third season of Four More Shots Please!, has been a big disappointment for me. The first season showcased CONNECTION and the third season depicted CONFUSION.

The web series first aired in the year 2019, and since then it has been loved all over the country. Hence, expectations for this new season were high and hopeful.

Background for newcomers

For all those who haven't seen any season yet, I would like to give a small background.

The series revolves around four best friends; Anjana, a lawyer, Damini, a journalist, Umang, a fitness trainer and Siddhi, daughter of filthy rich south Bombay parents.

The previous two seasons have shown various ups and downs in their lives and how they have together overcome those challenges.

The second season showcased COURAGE. Anjana overcomes a broken relationship, Siddhi accepts her body the way it is, Damini decides to publish her book in spite of controversies and Umang almost marries her love Samaira.

Third season had me hyped for days

When I found out about the third season, I really got excited. My husband and I saw it together, and we had the same reaction at the end of the series.

I won't disagree that the things depicted in season 3 are today's harsh realities, but we all are confused with relationships, career, ourselves and much more things but not to the extent it has shown in the series.

Sex has been shown as casual as if it's a daily affair. The series was based on friendship as shown in the last season.

A negative plot line and missed opportunity

The third season was so negative such as lying to your loved one, breaking hearts for your own selfish motive, insulting your widowed mother because she chose to live life freely; I mean these things actually made me annoyed while I was watching it.

I might be wrong, everyone has his/her own perspective, but for me season three has been a big mess.

The whole season transmitted such negative vibes. Luckily, when I discussed the series with my friends, they had the same opinion as mine.

Web Series have a huge impact on the people, and I am one of them, honestly.

Chapter 19

Live-in Or Married, Aftab Could Have Killed; So Stop Shaming Shraddha!

I respect the Government and the representatives working for all of us but some comments from the people who call themselves the government make me think about what mentality people have nowadays. Shraddha's murder is very unfortunate but using it to generalize a personal issue is disgusting. Union Minister of State for Housing and Urban Affairs, Kaushal Kishore, referring to the horrifying Shraddha Walker's murder case stated that "well-educated girls" are responsible for leaving their parents and hence being in a live-in relationship leads to crime.

God damn it, whether it's live-in or court marriage, will the person change? I will not take Shraddha's example, but if some person is violent or has the intention to kill, whether it's live-in or marriage, the person will eventually do so.

STOP blaming the victim – usually a woman

As far as live-in relationships are considered in general, it has nothing to do with education. Incidents like this are really unfortunate but generalizing it doesn't make sense at all. I come across so many headlines these days: woman killed for a cigarette, killed for chapati, killed for saying no to trip and many more unbelievable reasons.

Social media made a lot of memes on Shraddha Walkar but nothing on the killer Aftab Poonawalla, but why? "She did wrong, she left her parents, she was in a live-in relationship," she…, she… – yes, all talk is about the woman, but why is there no reference of the culprit? Why is the victim being blamed? Just because she is a female and hence a soft target?

I know some men will comment, "Don't become a feminist now!" Please understand that blaming a girl for everything is not justified, and as I have mentioned, if a person has a criminal motive, he will commit the crime irrespective of the relationship – whether married or in a live-in.

Parents do think for their children's good always, their decisions are in the best of our interest, but their child is not wrong every time. And parents can't shrug off responsibility to a child – after all, they decided to bring them into the world.

It is high time, we all should stop accusing women, start acclaiming them! Open your eyes to reality instead of being blind towards what's happening around us.

Chapter 20

Huma And Sonakshi's Double XL Reminds Me Of My Own Struggle Of Being A Fat Girl!

I saw the movie Double XL recently and it made me rewind my life. The first half of the movie highlights how a fat girl is being ignored and rejected at every step of her life and I could relate to it completely as I have gone through the same phase. The actresses Sonakshi Sinha and Huma Qureshi reflected how both of them struggled in their professional and personal life just because they were fat.

Some people will call you "chubby" or "healthy" instead of saying fat; I mean why is the word fat also taken in a negative sense? During my teenage years I took ayurvedic medicines owing to which I became overweight from being underweight. By saying overweight, I don't mean 60 or 70 kgs, my weight touched 95 kgs. Imagine a girl in her college weighing that much. Before seeing my face, everyone used to see my stomach. Every girl has a lot of dreams during her college days; mine were shattered because my weight took everything away from me.

I was shamed and rejected everywhere

I still can't forget that look from people; forget about people, my own family members. With time I got used to rejection. Rejection from somebody I loved, rejection from the job I aspired to and rejection from my own body at some point of time. Whenever I think about that time, I get scared. There was no way I could be loved by a man; hence my father started searching for matches for me. I was rejected back to back. There was a time where I abandoned all hope. Trust me; my mother said it on my face that this way you will never get married.

Today I am not the same, I shed almost 20 kgs to become a fit candidate and to my surprise I started to get many marriage matches. It's true that real life is far different than reel life. In the movie, Sonakshi and Huma succeed the way they are, but it was not the case with me. I had to deal with humiliation for a very long time until I made myself suitable for society's needs.

Today I am older and understand this better

When I look back today I feel it was me who didn't have the guts to face society. I was ashamed of my personality and therefore the world was.

To all the fat women out there, don't let anyone make you feel low, and if someone does, just say, "tere baap ka khati hoon kya".

About the Author

Smriti Malhotra

Smriti Malhotra works as a Secretary Incharge (Project Monitoring) in a Diplomatic Mission by profession and is a writer by passion. She started writing 20 years ago while she was in school, today she is a compiler, a published author and co-author in multiple anthologies.

Poetry is her first love. She has bagged numerous awards for her valuable contribution to the Literature World. She won the "Best Author" (Poetry category) Award 2021 by Priyasi Publications, Women Achiever Award 2021 by Priyasi Publications, Special Mention Award 2021 by Cherry Book Awards for the category "Best Author – Poetry 2021" and Poetic Caesura Book Awards 2.0 for the category "Poetry".

As destiny had something else stored for Smriti from poetry her forte changed to blogging. She started blogging - another interesting format of writing on renowned platforms like Youth ki Awaaz and Womensweb. She was an amateur in blogging when she started off in 2022 but today she has gained a lot of recognition on both the platforms. She has been upvoted for many blogs posted on Youth ki Awaaz and several have been editor's choice too on Womensweb.

She is a warrior, a survivor and a diligent girl, who is working generously towards her dreams. She is associated with poetry communities on Instagram as a Judge and content writer. Owing to her love for writing, she is crazy about collecting pens and stationary items. She believes that writing is powerful and aspires to reach the hearts of millions of people through her writing. When not working, she can be found in mountains or scrolling on instagram.

www.ingramcontent.com/pod-product-compliance
Lightning Source LLC
LaVergne TN
LVHW041551070526
838199LV00046B/1898